W9-AES-785

STRANGER ON THE SILK ROAD

A Story of Ancient China

by Jessica Gunderson

illustrated by Caroline Hu

PICTURE WINDOW BOOKS
Minneapolis, Minnesota

Editor: Shelly Lyons
Designer: Tracy Davies
Page Production: Michelle Biedscheid
Art Director: Nathan Gassman
Associate Managing Editor: Christianne Jones
The illustrations in this book were created with
brushed pen and ink.

Picture Window Books
151 Good Counsel Drive
P.O. Box 669
Mankato, MN 56002-0669
877-845-8392
www.picturewindowbooks.com

Library of Congress Cataloging-in-Publication Data
Gunderson, Jessica.
Stranger on the silk road : a story of ancient China /
by Jessica Gunderson ; illustrated by Caroline Hu.
p. cm. — (Read-it! chapter books: historical tales)
ISBN 978-1-4048-4736-1 (library binding)
1. China—History--Juvenile fiction. [1. China—
History—Fiction. 2. Silkworms—Fiction. 3. Silk—
Fiction.] I. Hu, Caroline, ill. II. Title.
PZ7.G963Si 2008
[Fic]—dc22   2008006308

c.1

TABLE OF CONTENTS

WORDS TO KNOW

Confucius—a Chinese philosopher whose teachings still influence many Asian citizens and other people around the world

Great Wall of China—a 4,000-mile (6,400-kilometer) wall that stretches across northern China

Han Dynasty (206 B.C.–A.D. 220)—Liu Bang defeated the Qin Dynasty in 206 B.C., and the Han Dynasty began; Chang'an was the capital during the Han Dynasty, and it was also the starting point of the Silk Road

merchant—someone who buys and sells things for profit

Silk Road—a series of roads that were a major trade route for merchants in ancient China

INTRODUCTION

167 B.C.—Han Dynasty

Confucius, the great Chinese thinker, said: "Speak enough to make the point, and then leave it at that."

I often heard the words of Confucius repeated, but I did not listen. I never listened. I was a young girl, and I was too busy talking to hear anyone else.

"You are always talking, Song Sun," said my mother.

"Always talking and never listening," agreed my father.

"You are wrong," I said.

But I knew they were right. I was often talking and rarely listening. I liked to argue that I didn't listen because no one ever listened to me—no one, that is, except my little sister, Song Ki, and the stranger who appeared out of nowhere one day.

One day, Song Ki and I were traveling along the Silk Road to the village. We rode in a horse-drawn cart piled high with silk. We were carrying the silk for our father to trade.

Ki was crying as usual. She'd been crying for a year, ever since her feet were bound with tight bandages.

"My feet hurt," she whimpered.

"When I had my feet bound, I did not cry as much as you," I told her. "In order to be beautiful, you must bind your feet. Remember that, and the pain will go away."

In ancient China, little girls wrapped
their feet to keep them from growing
big and ugly. Small feet were considered
beautiful. Mine were tiny. Only the
very rich bound their feet. My family
was wealthy, but my parents wished
me to marry into even greater wealth.
Someday, I would be able to lure a rich
husband with my tiny, lovely feet.

"Will my feet ever stop hurting, Sun?" Ki asked.

"Yes. When you are 6 years old," I answered.

"But that is a year away!" Ki wailed.

"A year will go fast," I said. "In a few years, I will have to go live with a husband and his parents. I will have to say goodbye to you."

Ki sniffled.

"Look!" I cried, pointing down the
road. "I can see the village."

We stopped at the edge of the road
to let our horse rest. Farmers hurried
past, on their way to the village to sell
their goods to traveling merchants. The
merchants would take their goods along
the Silk Road to faraway lands. Silk was
the most popular thing to sell. China
was the only place where silk was made.
Silk making was a Chinese secret.

A man on a horse appeared at the top of the hill. He was a shadow against the bright morning sun. His silk robe shimmered in the light. His hair was in a ponytail at the top of his head, the way many Chinese men wore it. As he drew nearer, I noticed there was something strange about his eyes.

Ki clutched my hand.

The strangeness disappeared when the man smiled at us. He got off his horse and wiped his brow.

"We are going to the village to trade our silk," I told him. "My father is a silk merchant."

The stranger leaned forward, listening to my words. I did not notice the greedy gleam in his eyes. I kept talking. I did not know his plan.

CHAPTER TWO

"May I please look at your silk?" the
stranger asked.

He reached into our cart and unfolded
a roll of silk. "What lovely silk!" he
exclaimed. "It is so rich and colorful."

"My family makes the best silk in the
land," I told him proudly.

He studied the fabric in his hands. Meanwhile, I studied his hair. It was coarse and dull, not shiny like mine. As he moved his head, his hair fell across his forehead. He tried to hold it down.

"My father is wealthy," I told him. "But when he was a boy, he had to work in the silk fields."

"Where are the fields?" the stranger asked. He was still holding his hair, which flopped in the wind.

I pointed south. "Oh, over there," I told him. "My father made my sister and me learn to make silk, too."

Ki tugged on my arm. But I ignored her. She only wanted to moan about her feet, I was sure.

"You know how to make silk?" the stranger asked. He was so excited he let go of his hair, and it flopped onto his forehead again.

"Yes," I said. "But it's not very exciting. I would rather tell you all about my new slippers—"

"Where do you find silk threads?" he interrupted.

Ki tugged my arm so hard she almost ripped my sleeve. I kept talking.

"First, you have to have mulberry trees—lots of them. Mulberry leaves are all the silkworm will eat."

"The silkworm!" cried the stranger. "There is a worm that makes silk?"

I sighed, feeling impatient. Didn't this man know anything? I thought everyone in China knew how to make silk.

"Yes. The worm spins its cocoon with soft threads. Then you dip the cocoon in hot water to get rid of the stickiness."

"I see," said the stranger. "Then you pull apart the cocoons and use the threads?" he asked.

I watched him. There was something strange about his eyes and his hair.

Ki kicked me. But her feet were so sore that it hurt her worse than it hurt me. Tears flooded her eyes.

"Ki is crying about her feet," I told the stranger. "When I was a little girl—"

"And how do you turn the threads into silk?" he asked.

His horse pawed at the ground. I
thought there was something strange
about the horse, too. What was it?

"We spin the small threads into thick
threads," I explained. "Then we dye the
threads different colors and weave them
together to make fabric."

The stranger clapped his hands
together. "And the worms?" he asked.
"Are they crawling about in the fields?"

But he didn't wait for my answer. He didn't even bow to me like a Chinese gentleman should. Instead, he hopped onto his horse. He waved one hand as he galloped away.

As the stranger and his horse rode into the distance, I realized what was so strange about the horse. It had no tail.

CHAPTER THREE

"That man scared me!" Ki said, shivering. "You shouldn't talk to strangers, Sun."

We were approaching the village. The market bustled with people.

"He listened to me," I said. "No one else listens to me, except you."

Then I saw a familiar face in the crowd. "Look! There's Father!" I cried.

My father rushed toward us. "Where have you been?" he scolded. "I must sell this silk today." He looked up at the sun. "And it will soon be tomorrow!"

"I am sorry," I said. I should have known he would be angry. His silk meant everything to him.

Our father had once been a poor man, as poor as the peasants who worked in our silk fields.

"When I was young, I did not have time to talk as much as you, Sun," he often told us. "Or to cry as much as you, Ki. I was always working in the fields."

It was unusual for a poor peasant like my father to become wealthy. But my father was a hard worker. He studied different silkworms and figured out which ones made the best silk. When he shared his discovery with a landowner, the landowner was grateful. When the rich man died, he gave my father his entire silk business.

Now my father is a wealthy merchant.
That is why his silk is so precious to him.

He was still glaring at me, waiting for
an answer.

"We stopped to rest," I said.

Ki added, "And there was also a
strange man—"

I pinched her under her sleeve. She
howled. My father ignored us and
wheeled the cart toward his shop.

As we followed, Ki said to me, "He was strange. He had funny hair—"

Just then, I realized why the man had looked so strange. His hair was horsehair, cut from his very own horse! He had made a wig from his horse's tail! The stranger was not Chinese! And he was going to take the silk secret and spread it to other lands!

Misery swept over me. Because of me, the Chinese silk secret was in danger. Because of me, our family would probably lose everything.

That night, I had terrible dreams. I woke long before dawn, my heart beating fast. The moon overhead shone as white as a silk cocoon.

I have to find the stranger before it is too late, I thought, peering out the window. As I watched, a man passed by on his horse. The horse had no tail.

I ran out the door and into the street. "Stop!" I yelled. "Thief!"

The stranger turned and saw me.

"It's too late," he cackled with an evil grin. "I know the secret."

He held up his hand. In the moonlight, I saw dozens of silkworms squirming in his palm. He cackled again and kicked his horse into a gallop. I ran after him as fast as I could. But my feet were too small. I could only hobble.

A woman leaned out of her window as I passed. "Stop that racket!" she said.

"But that man is stealing the secrets of the Chinese people!" I gasped.

The woman squinted at me. Then she laughed and said, "Oh, it is only you, Song Sun. I do not need to listen to you. You are always talking about nothing."

"Please!" I begged. But she just turned away.

I knew I could not stop the stranger on my own. But I could talk and talk and no one would believe me. How could I make people listen?

Then an idea came to me. I would have to take a big risk, but it might work.

CHAPTER FOUR

Just before dawn, I saddled my father's horse. Father would be angry when he found the horse missing. I hoped he would forgive me when he found out why I had borrowed it. I turned the horse in the direction the stranger had gone.

Zhang Si-Kai, a friend of my father's, was outside feeding his chickens. When he saw me, he bowed.

"Hello, Sun!" he called. "Where are you going?"

I did not answer. I kept the horse at a steady pace.

"What?" he asked. "You have nothing to say?"

I did not answer.

Mr. Zhang shook his head in disbelief.

Then he began to run along the road beside me. "Sun! Is something wrong?" he asked. "Why aren't you talking?"

Still I said nothing.

He stopped running. But I soon heard a horse's hooves behind me. Mr. Zhang was following me.

"She is not talking!" he announced to everyone we passed.

We passed the woman I had seen last
night. When Mr. Zhang told her that I
was not speaking, she looked amazed.

"Song Sun not talking?" she asked.
"What has happened?"

She got on her horse and joined
Mr. Zhang. "Song Sun is not talking!"
they both shouted to anyone who
would listen.

A man and his son got on their horses and followed. Then an old woman and her dog followed. By the time I reached the edge of the village, a hundred people were following me.

We passed from one village to the next. I never said a word. And people followed. Sometimes they whispered to each other. But most of the time, they were silent, waiting for me to speak. But I did not speak.

How I longed to talk! Words bubbled
inside of me, wanting to come out. But
I kept them inside. I remembered the
words of Confucius, "Speak enough to
make the point, and then leave it at
that." I kept repeating those words in my
head. And I felt calm.

We rode past lakes and streams, past mountains and fields of rice. We rode all day and all night. We rode and rode without stopping. Soon, we rode so far north that fields of rice had turned into fields of wheat. In the distance, stretching like a snake over the mountains, was a giant stone wall. We had reached the Great Wall of China. This was the end of Chinese lands.

My heart sank. If the stranger had already passed beyond the wall and into other lands, it was too late.

Then I saw a figure ahead of us. It was a man with flopping hair—and a horse with no tail. He looked back at us as we approached. The hundreds of hooves from our horses echoed like thunder in the hills.

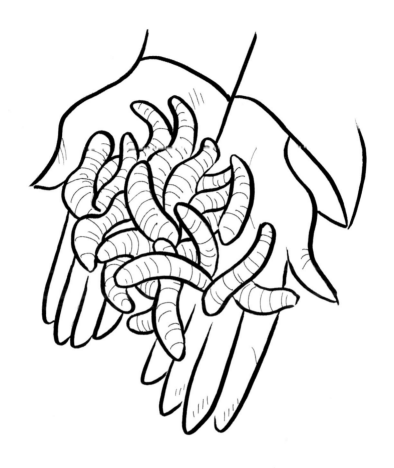

I saw him reach into his bag. He
pulled out his hands and cupped them
together. Inside his hands, I knew, he
held silkworms. I stopped my horse. The
crowd behind me stopped, too.

I raised my hand to point at the stranger. Then I spoke the first words I had spoken in days. The crowd stopped breathing and leaned forward to listen.

"That man," I said, "has stolen the Chinese secret of silk making!"

CHAPTER FIVE

The stranger trembled. His face flushed.
He looked at the crowd of people
surrounding him. Then he smiled.

"I have stolen nothing," he said. "I am a good Chinese man. I have always known how to make silk."

"Look at what he holds in his hands," I said.

Fear lit the stranger's eyes. He urged his horse to back away from the crowd.

"She is just a little girl who talks a lot," he said, holding his cupped hands together. "She has made it up."

Mr. Zhang glared at the stranger. He leaned forward in his saddle. His horse leaped forward, charging at the stranger.

The stranger's eyes grew wide. His horse's eyes did, too. Then the horse reared in fright. The stranger tumbled to the ground. His horse hair flew from his head. The wind lifted it like a kite and blew it over the Great Wall. He landed on his back, dropping his handful of silkworms. They fell on him like rain, squirming on his face and chest.

The man no longer looked Chinese.
Golden-yellow curls clung to his
scalp. His silk robe had fallen off, too.
Underneath it he wore funny-looking
brown pants and a shirt of rags.

"Thief!" cried one woman.

"Kill him!" roared another.

"No!" I held up my hand. The shouts fell silent. "We will take him to my father. He will know what to do."

I stared down at the stranger. He
looked at me, and his eyes twinkled with
tears. He wasn't much older than me. He
was just a frightened young man.

I led the crowd back to our village.
We never let the stranger out of our sight.
Sometimes I saw him looking at me with
gratitude. And sometimes I let him share
my rice when we stopped to rest and
eat. He was a thief, but he couldn't be
entirely bad. No one was.

CHAPTER SIX

My parents rushed to greet me when we
arrived in the village. Little Ki hugged
me so tightly I couldn't breathe. Her eyes
were red from crying.

"This time it isn't about my feet," she said.

Zhang Si-Kai said to my father, "Your daughter is a heroine. She has saved China from ruin."

I hung my head. "No," I replied. "I am the one who put China in danger."

As I told my story, my father kept stroking the silk he carried in his arms.

I understood. He was imagining what it would have been like to lose what he loved.

My mother was very angry. "You see, Sun?" she said. "Now you understand where all your talking will lead."

Mr. Zhang broke in. "And now for the stranger's punishment!" he said. "What will it be?"

My father stroked his beard, staring
at the stranger. "So, you love silk?"
he asked.

The stranger's face grew pale. "Yes,"
he whispered.

"Do you want to learn more about
silk?" my father asked.

The stranger looked at his feet. "Yes,"
he replied.

My father nodded. "Then you will work for us," he said.

I gasped, my mother gasped, and Ki gasped, too.

The stranger stared at my father. "But my punishment?" he asked.

"You will not return to your home country," my father said. "That is punishment enough."

And that is how the stranger came to work for us. He has been a good worker, too. And kind. He is almost like a brother to me, even though he has yellow hair. We call him Kho-Kho. He told us he was from a land far away, where people paid a lot of money for silk.

Whenever I ask him if he is sad because he can't go home, he shakes his head. "I have no family there anymore," he says. "And I love China."

I do not talk much anymore. I have
listened to the words of Confucius. I
speak enough to make the point, and
then leave it at that. Besides, little Ki does
enough talking for all of us. Now that
her feet no longer hurt her, she spends
her time talking instead of crying.

I often hear my parents telling her what they once told me. "You are always talking, Ki," my mother says.

"Always talking and never listening," grumbles my father.

The stranger and I grin at each other.
But we don't say a word.

AFTERWORD

Merchants traded their goods along the Silk Road for thousands of years. The Silk Road was more than just one road, however. It consisted of dozens of intersecting routes that crisscrossed China. The most-traveled part of the Silk Road stretched from the Chinese city of Chang'an (known today as Xian) all the way to ancient Rome.

Despite its name, merchants on the Silk Road carried more than just silk. They carried other goods such as pottery, tea, gunpowder, magnetic compasses, and jade. These items were native to China. The Chinese had invented gunpowder and magnetic compasses and were the first to make pottery with a spinning wheel. When these items became known to the rest of the world, they were in high demand.

Silk was very popular in Europe and other parts of Asia. Kings and queens paid large amounts of money for silk clothing. People loved the rich colors, beautiful patterns, and soft feel of the fabric. For thousands of years, the process of making silk remained a secret, known only to the Chinese people.

As travel and trade increased, Chinese people began settling in other lands. They took the secret of silk production with them. In about 200 B.C.,

Chinese immigrants took the secret to Korea, but kept it among themselves. By A.D. 300, India was raising silkworms. By the 13th century, the knowledge of silk production had spread to Italy and other European countries.

Though the world now knows the secret of silk making, China remains the leader in silk production. Bolts of silk and other goods still travel on parts of the Silk Road today.

ON THE WEB

FactHound offers a safe, fun way to find Web sites related to topics in this book. All of the sites on FactHound have been researched by our staff.

1. Visit *www.facthound.com*
2. Type in this special code: 1404847367
3. Click on the FETCH IT button.

Your trusty FactHound will fetch the best sites for you!

LOOK FOR MORE *READ-IT!* READER CHAPTER BOOKS: HISTORICAL TALES:

The Actor, the Rebel, and the Wrinkled Queen
The Blue Stone Plot
The Boy Who Cried Horse
The Emperor's Painting
The Gold in the Grave
The Jade Dragon
The Lion's Slave
The Magic and the Mummy
The Maid, the Witch, and the Cruel Queen
The Phantom and the Fisherman
The Plot on the Pyramid
The Prince, the Cook, and the Cunning King
The Secret Warning
The Shepherd and the Racehorse
The Terracotta Girl
The Thief, the Fool, and the Big Fat King
The Torchbearer
The Tortoise and the Dare
The Town Mouse and the Spartan House